I0720898

THE ZIGZAG PAPERS

~ or ~

WHO WANTS WANDA WASTED?

Other books by David Hedges

Petty Frogs on the Potomac (1997)
The Wild Bunch (1998)
Brother Joe (2000)
Steens Mountain Sunrise: Poems
of the Northern Great Basin (2004)
Selected Sonnets (2006)
A Funny Thing Happened on My Way
to a Geology Degree (2011)
Prospects of Life After Birth: Memoir
in Poetry and Prose (2019)
The Changer (2021)
Trump Über Alles: Rhymes
for Trying Times (2022)

THE ZIGZAG PAPERS

~ or ~

WHO WANTS WANDA WASTED?

An Inspector François Poulet of Interpol
Attempted Murder Mystery

~ by ~

DAVID HEDGES

ROAD'S END PRESS

The Zigzag Papers or Who Wants Wanda Wasted: An Inspector François
Poulet of Interpol Attempted Murder Mystery
by David Hedges

Road's End Press
326 Pearl Street
Oregon City, Oregon 97045

To order copies, visit roadsendpress.com

Cover design by *Erik Wilson*
Illustrations by *Jim Agpalza*
Design and compositing by *Andrew Hedges*
Proofreading by *Valerie Witte*
Project management by *Erin Hedges*

Library of Congress Control Number: 2022950832

ISBN: 978-1-7366102-4-4

Ebook version available

Printed in the United States of America

I dedicate this bit of whimsey

to Inspector Jacques Clouseau

of the Sûreté nationale

Cast of Characters

Armand DuBois, sous-chef at the Grand Hotel in Zürich, Switzerland, soon to become known as Inspector François Poulet of Interpol.

Wanda Fuller, Zigzag, Oregon postmistress (identifies as mail person), nudist, and author of *The Book of Love.*

Edgar Hoover, Government Camp, Oregon private eye, who keeps his one good eye on Wanda.

Chief MacDonald Cook of the twelve-man Zigzag Volunteer Police Force, all of whom have the hots for Wanda.

Rudyard Ripley, general manager of Ripley's River Resort, big game hunter, hypnotist, and Wanda's third husband.

Marva Luce, owner of Rudyard Ripley and Ripley's River Resort, and Wanda's all-time archenemy.

Ben Wa, editor of *The Zigzag Rag,* a weekly (bi-weekly, monthly, whatever) newspaper, and Wanda's fifth husband.

Deputy Dexter Dippe of the Clackamas County Sheriff's Department. "Call me Dex. Rhymes with sex."

Rhonda, Wanda's identical twin sister, who is "seen from time to time" by Wanda's ex-husbands.

Earnest Hummingbird, Boring, Oregon lepidopterist, and the first of Wanda's husbands.

Fritz Jerrold, German ski instructor at Mount Hood's Timberline Lodge and Wanda's husband Number Two.

Milo Graham, ebullient Zigzag poet who is madly in love with
Wanda. "Some would say simply mad."

Hobo Hooker, corporate dropout and itinerant fiddler, who
lives in the crawl space beneath Wanda's house.

Général Henri Malaise (Retired), infamous French World War
Two hero, and Wanda's fourth husband.

Anna Graham, Milo's older sister and caregiver, who suffers
from a rare form of anxiety disorder.

Buck Fuller, owner and manager of the Rhododendron Limb
Company, and Wanda's sixth and last husband.

Cast of Creators

David Hedges, Oregon author, poet, humorist, and social, polit-
ical, and environmental tub-thumper.

Jim Agpalza, artist extraordinaire, who lifted off from a distant
galaxy and landed outside Portland, Oregon.

ARMAND DuBOIS

Prologue

29 June

Dear Uncle Claude, I have arrived this day at the village of Zigzag, Oregon, on the American West. Here I shall rest three days at Ripley's River Resort, a quaint hostelry recommended for its peaceful views. I notice from the menu a 'formidable' fricassee de poulet. I must see to believe. So, I shall post this now, and write more after I inspect the poulet—if I survive!

Love, Armand

WANDA FULLER

EDGAR HOOVER

CHIEF MACDONALD COOK

1

Wanda sensed something was dreadfully wrong. Her captor's cage had landed smack on the trail between her back porch and the river at the precise moment she stepped beneath it. But who would do such a weird thing? And why? She gripped a pair of bars and peered out.

"Rhonda!" she screamed, recoiling in horror from the double image of her identical twin sister. But no, it was her own face!—reflected in the twin mirrors of Edgar Hoover's silvered sunglasses.

"Ugh!"

Edgar raised his glasses and wiped the rim of his good eye with a white-gloved forefinger.

"Anyone who observes your habits, as I do," he burbled, his words a raft of sympathy in a sea of lust, "knows you step outside every evening at six for a quick dip in the Zigzag, wearing only a smile and a pair of Army boots."

"Cut the crap, Edgar! Get me out of here!"

Whirrr-click.

"And stop taking pictures!"

Edgar, who was listed in the Government Camp phone book under "Private Eye," spent nine-tenths of every waking hour keeping an eye on Wanda. His camera, concealed in his other eye, the glass eye, gave itself away again.

Whirrr-click.

"Please, Edgar? Pretty please?"

Edgar adjusted the belt on his rumpled trench coat, staring first at his bare feet, then at the fir boughs above.

"Oh, all right," she sighed, striking his favorite pose.

Whirrr-click.

Grinning, he wrapped his puffy paws around a bar and

threw his weight away from the cage. The bar popped free. He pedaled back fifty paces and tumbled, flailing, into the frigid Zigzag. "W-Wanda m-my d-dove!" he cried as the current caught and swept him away.

"Ugh!"

She slipped from the cage and dashed up the path. Five steps shy of the porch, a black leather jackboot shot from behind a tree, caught her below the knees, and sent her sprawling. Chief MacDonald Cook, whose Zigzag Volunteer Police Force boasted "More Cops Per Capita" in red, white, and blue blazing neon, tucked his swagger stick under his arm and helped her up.

"All in the line of duty," he chuckled, picking twigs and bits of moss from her otherwise flawless skin.

She planted a knee in his crotch. He doubled over. "Psychomotor seizure," she apologized sheepishly.

"I'm here…," he wheezed, "to investigate… an attempt… on your life."

"Woo!" said Wanda. "So that's what's going on!"

The chief straightened up and leaned against a tree. "I received an anonymous tip. *Honest.*"

She reached down to unlace her boots. Glancing between her knees, she spied all twelve Zigzag Volunteers projecting from the forest floor like stalks of blue asparagus.

"Blow!" she bellowed.

They scattered.

"Line o' duty," mumbled the chief.

"Bull!"

RUDYARD RIPLEY

MARVA LUCE

2

"Double whoa!" roared Rudyard Ripley, bending close when Edgar's glasses flashed silver from his salmon net. *"You're* a prize!"

Edgar sneezed, coughed, and blew his nose without benefit of tissue, in the process taking twelve tight shots of Rudyard's nostrils.

"Drat!" snapped Rudyard. "It's *alive!*" He dropped Edgar's head on a rock.

When Edgar again opened his eye, it was only to face the cruel crow's-feet of Marva Luce, owner of Rudyard Ripley and his River Resort. "I'm dead!" he croaked, closing his eye.

She resisted her urge to chop him into bite-sized bits. "Lucky for you," she grumbled, grinding her teeth.

Marva was the last of six children conceived by Karl and Lillian Kruse . . . or, the first of six children conceived by Lester and Lillian Luce. All three parents, plus each couple's five pedigreed offspring and their respective husbands, wives, and children, had died of food poisoning following a family reunion, leaving her the sole heir to twelve estates. Simply by being Marva, she had picked up seventeen million dollars, plus personal effects.

Among those effects was a modest collection of rubber underwear once worn by her closest Luce sister, Antoinette, on doctor's orders. From the magic moment of discovery, Marva wore nothing else. Her new interest soon drew her on a worldwide search for the ultimate in rubber accessories, one of which, a thirty-foot replica of a seaweed whip, she now twirled above her head.

Again, Edgar opened his eye. "Edgar Hoo—"

"Aieeeeee!" shrieked Marva, dancing in a tight circle, groping

for the blowgun dart planted in her flank. Rudyard tried to sneak between trees. She wrapped her whip around his neck. His eyes bulged. His lips turned purple.

"Dildohead!" she shrilled. "You've landed a walleyed government agent!"

"And I'm Marlin Perkins!" rasped Rudyard, frantically uncoiling the whip. "He's a *private* agent, retired when the government accidentally erased his memory. Although that does sound fishy, doesn't it? But we needn't worry. He's only after Wanda."

Hearing the name of her absolute all-time archenemy, Marva trimmed small limbs from every tree for thirty feet around.

BEN WA

<h1 style="text-align:center">3</h1>

Wanda sensed something was dreadfully wrong. Her struggle to unsnap the clasps on her antigravity boots had drained her strength. Try as she might, she was unable to free her feet. A wolf whistle pierced the drumbeat pounding in her ears. Turning, she looked upside down into Edgar's smiling eye.

"Ugh!"

"W-watch the b-birdie," he chirped, tottering in his soggy trench coat.

Whirrr-click.

A squad car squealed into the driveway and screeched to a halt. Chief Cook ran to assist Edgar in lowering Wanda. His passenger, Ben Wa, editor of *The Zigzag Rag,* scribbled furiously on a spiral notepad.

Safely inside, Wanda stretched out on her polar bear rug. The chief escorted Ben and Edgar out. Slamming the door, he pulled his pearl-handled revolver and pounced on Wanda. She rolled over and jumped up, dumping him flat on his back.

"Ugh!"

The chief found Ben in the driveway. "We're in a pickle here, Ben. Somebody's got it in for Wanda. What'll we do?"

"Got a hot tip, Mac. Big-shot cop down at Ripley's River Resort. Swiss cheese named Poulet, on inspection tour."

The chief pushed back his cap. "Inspector François Poulet of Interpol? I thought he was *fiction.*"

"So. Truth is stranger than fiction."

"Why, I've read every episode in his career! Ben, how in the hell—"

"Ah. Easy as falling off a log. Saw his postal card at the front desk."

"Anybody else get a gander?"

Ben shook his head. His eyes brimmed behind round, wire-rimmed spectacles.

The chief rubbed his beefy hands. "Promise you won't spill the beans."

Ben kicked a rock. "Now, Mac, remember freedom of the press, guaranteed in the Bill of Rights. Reads as follows—"

The chief pulled his revolver.

"Promise!"

4

Chief Cook studied the guest register, running his finger up and down for the fifth time. "No Poulet?" he puzzled.

The desk clerk studied his manicured nails. "You might try our dinner menu," he yawned.

"How about a Swiss?"

"We have a Swiss."

"On the menu?"

"On the guest list. Armand DuBois."

"DuBois. An alias."

"Yes, of course."

"He is Inspector François Poulet of Interpol."

"And I am Hercule Poirot," clucked the clerk, flapping a hand toward the dining room.

5

"Inspector François Poulet?"

"Pardon?"

"The jig's up. Your cover's blown."

Armand sat back and studied the square, pink face casting a shadow across his soup du jour, assuring himself that he, a Swiss sous-chef on holiday in the American West, was in little, if any, danger.

"This jig you speak of . . ." he offered cautiously.

"Don't try to duck, Poulet."

"Duck? Poulet?"

"I'll be frank. There's a lot at stake here. I've got egg on my face. If I make a hash of it, my goose is cooked."

"Goose?"

"I'm dancing on a hot griddle. So don't waffle. I need your brain."

"My brain?" Armand glanced about for his waiter.

"Sorry to put the bite on you. For me, this is a tough nut to crack. But for you, Inspector, it's a piece of cake. Meat and potatoes. So, what's the good word?"

"Soup." Armand raised his jiggling spoon, but the soup spilled over the sides.

"Are you game, Inspector?"

"Perhaps yes—" At the sight of the chief's pearl-handled revolver, he nodded vigorously. "Yes, yes, of course! And you are—?"

"Chief Cook, Zigzag Police. Call me Mac."

Armand offered a perspiring palm. "Armand DuBois. Sous-chef. Grand Hotel, Zürich."

The chief jerked his hand away and wiped it the length of his thigh. "Sweat!"

"This game you speak of..."

The chief whipped a chair around and straddled it. "Some turkey," he confided, "is trying to toast Wanda Fuller's buns."

Armand reared back. "First... who is Wanda Fuller?"

"*Where—*" boomed the chief.

Armand's waiter dropped his tray at their feet.

"—have you been hiding?" whispered the chief.

"Switzerland?"

The chief rolled his eyes. "She's the Wanda who wrote The Book of Love... the runaway bestseller! She's our local post-mistress."

"I see," sighed Armand, watching the waiter scrape his fricassee de poulet from the parquet floor. He had not eaten since a meager breakfast on the flight from San Francisco.

"What's more, she's a peach, and she walks around as naked as a peeled banana. Well, Inspector, what do you say? Will you take the case?"

"Call me François."

6

Wanda sat cross-legged on her polar bear rug, watching as Armand peeked under her four-posted featherbed, around her antique wicker armchairs, into her ceramic urns and among her dried weeds and peacock feathers, up her river-cobble chimney, down her quaint tin kitchen sink, and behind her bathroom door. Satisfied, he settled cross-legged to the plank floor, inches from the bear's bared teeth. Glancing down, he sprang to his feet.

"Now start at the top," he blustered, pointing to the peeled log ceiling beams, "and we shall get to the bottom!"

She shrugged. "It's a mystery to me."

The chief slapped Armand on the back. "Hot dog, François! Why, that's your bread and butter!"

Armand's stomach grumbled. "Yes. Now, I should like to examine the lay of your land. These bungles, I believe, occurred alfresco." He helped her up.

The chief cupped a hand. "I think he means outdoors. You gotta watch these foreigners." He stuck his tongue in her ear.

She swung sharply about, bouncing an elbow off his solar plexus and hooking Armand's arm on the rebound. "My rubber boots are by the door, Inspector. Have you ever tried walking barefoot during slug season?"

Armand shrugged. "Which season is that?"

"That's when you can't even take a step," she gushed, slipping into her boots, "without coming down on something squishy that oozes up between your toes, all sticky and slimy and gooey, and won't wash off, and sometimes spurts—"

The chief clapped his hands to his mouth and ran for the bathroom.

"Now we can be alone," she laughed, leading Armand out

the door and into the night.

A sprinkling of stars sparkled through pinpricks in the thick canopy of fir and cedar needles and alder leaves. The rhythmic croaks and chirps of frogs and crickets pulsed like the drones of cellos and violas over the river's random babble.

Wanda pointed into the trees. "That's where I got hung up in my gravity boots."

"I see," he replied, gazing into the startling darkness.

She took his hand and led him to the trail between her back porch and the river. "There's where the cage dropped." He nodded.

She poked him in the ribs. "The *cage?*"

"I see."

"Then there were the poison caterpillars."

"Tell me about the caterpillars. Did you eat any?"

"*Eat* any?"

"Poison caterpillars."

"They poison you with their little spines."

"Did you touch any?"

"Why would I do a stupid thing like that?"

"Tell me about the caterpillars."

"I knew what they were because my first husband collects poison caterpillars. He calls that *living dangerously.*"

"What do *you* call it?"

"Bull."

"I see. And where is your first husband?"

"Boring."

"*Where* is your first husband?"

"Boring. A town southwest of here. But it couldn't have been Earnest."

"Earnest?"

"Hummingbird. My first husband. He wouldn't harm a fly. Of course, he does some pretty weird things with *butter*flies."

"Is there a second husband?"

"Fritz Jerrold. A ski instructor up at Timberline Lodge. But he's chicken."

Armand's stomach growled. "Chicken?"

"He broke his leg six years ago, and he's kept it in a cast ever since. It's got hinges on it, so he only has to wear it during working hours. And when he's down hustling in the Blue Ox."

"Hustling?"

"And drinking. He drinks a lot."

"The blue ox?"

"It's a great watering hole."

"He hustles in a watering hole?"

"Anything with tits."

"I see."

They started back. He was about to ask if she had a third husband when a rope closed about his ankle and he was yanked up into the trees.

7

Wanda sensed something was dreadfully wrong. Edgar had failed to pop up from the bushes. And slug talk usually put the chief out of commission for a few minutes at most. Now, even the crickets were still. She took a tentative step. A twig snapped. She froze. Another twig snapped. Suddenly the air erupted with thuds and smacks, and the crackles of someone, or some *thing,* stumbling off through the underbrush.

"Inspector?"

"Here," he whispered.

"Where . . . is here?"

"Promise you won't jump?"

"Promise."

"Here." He touched her shoulder. She jumped into his arms.

"Where were you, Inspector?"

"In a tree. But a simple slipknot shall never hold Armand DuBois."

"Who is Armand DuBois?"

"Armand DuBois is . . . "

"Yes?"

"The founder of the Swiss Boy Scouts."

"You were a Boy Scout?"

"Yes."

"Kiss me."

"Boy Scouts do not kiss."

"Bull!" She overwhelmed him with her lips. He sank slowly—only to rise as Chief Cook burst from the back door and stumbled down the stairs.

"Inspector! *Inspector!*"

Armand dropped Wanda.

"Inspector!"

The chief knocked Armand to the ground and fell on him.

"Inspector—?"

"Chief—?"

"What in the hell happened?"

"I went up in a tree. Then I came down. *On* someone. That someone ran away. Then Wanda jumped into my arms. Then you shouted and I dropped her. Then you knocked me down and fell on me. That's all I know."

"Wanda?"

"François was caught in a slipknot. Then there was this terrible racket. Then someone touched me and I jumped. And François caught me. And then you yelled. And François dropped me. And you ran into François."

"Chief?"

"Beats me. One minute I was chucking my guts out, and the next minute I was working my way out of a nifty set of half hitches. Here—" He switched on his six-cell flashlight.

"Up!" piped Armand, shielding his eyes against the startling brightness.

The beam caught a limp form dangling by one leg from a snare.

"Edgar!" cried Wanda.

"He has but one eye," observed Armand.

"There's a camera in his other eye," snickered the chief.

"Then his camera is missing."

"Let's hope to hell it's his camera!"

They lowered Edgar, still wet from his river tumble, and brought him around.

"Wh-what h-hit m-me?" he sniffled. His teeth chattered like castanets.

"*Who* hit you," corrected Armand.

"Did you get a gander?" asked the chief.

"I g-got a p-picture!"

"Bull," said Wanda.

The chief sent Edgar home in his squad car, then escorted Armand and Wanda to the cabin. "Got to trot," he said, adjusting his cap. "Poker night at the Elks."

"But there's a murderer after me!" pleaded Wanda.

"François here can handle your beef. Chop-chop."

"But—!" blurted Armand.

"But *what?*" puzzled Wanda.

His stomach gurgled. "I have to eat something."

"I make a mean omelet," she said, brushing fir needles from his shoulders.

"I *know* you can handle a *chick*," chuckled the chief, nudging Armand's ribs with an elbow. "I've read all your books. Some parts more than others." He strolled out the door, humming, cracking his knuckles.

A moment later, he poked his head back inside, grinning sheepishly. "Kinda laid an egg," he mumbled. "Plumb forgot. Edgar. My car."

Wanda swept her keys off the mantel and threw them across the room. The chief caught them and clumped back down the steps. The car door slammed.

"Alone at last," sighed Wanda.

"Yes," replied Armand.

They touched fingertips. The sky lit up. The cabin trembled. A thunderous rumbling rang in their ears. Then silence, punctuated by a distant hissing.

"*Woo!*" warbled Wanda.

❧ 8 ❧

The chief stumbled up the steps and staggered in. His hands and face were caked with greasy soot. His fringe of singed hair stood straight out. His uniform hung from his slumped frame like a tattered battle flag. He still gripped the steering wheel.

"Your cream puff just turned into a squeezed lemon," he mumped. "Mind if I . . . use your phone?"

Wanda switched on the porch light and peered out the open door at her once-shiny white Mustang convertible. The hood and trunk lids stood at attention. The doors leaned at odd angles. Steam shot from the radiator. Black smoke billowed from the carburetor and the blazing tires. Strips of dirty gray canvas festooned the tree branches. Shatterproof glass littered the gravel driveway, glittering like cat's-eye marbles.

"Ugh!"

Armand joined her at the door. "Perhaps we should call the police."

She waggled a hand at the chief. "He's right there."

"Perhaps we should . . . seek outside help."

"That's you."

"Perhaps there is some . . . higher authority."

"The Clackamas County Sheriff's Department?"

"Yes."

The chief switched off the phone and rearranged his uniform to cover the flamingo-pink silk peeking from behind his toothless zipper. "This rhubarb has mushroomed into a witches' brew. What's your best advice, François?"

"He thinks we should call the cops."

Sirens wailed. Red and blue lights flashed. Squad cars of a dozen makes and models, fuel-efficient and otherwise, filled the driveway and spilled out onto Highway 26. The Zigzag

Volunteers converged on the door and squeezed through in one pop, exhaling in unison.

"Atten-*hut!*" barked the chief.

The Volunteers shifted from foot to foot.

"I want . . . and don't anyone dare take a step back . . . a Volunteer to drive Inspector Poulet down to Ripley's—"

They shrank as one toward the door.

"—and two to guard Wanda."

They surged forward, waving wild elbows and arms.

"*Owwwww!*" yowled the chief. "Oooooo! Owwwww!"

"Atten-*HUT!*" roared Armand.

The Volunteers turned board stiff.

"What else do Boy Scouts do?" cooed Wanda, drawing close and ruffling Armand's blond waves.

He smiled wistfully. "Go to bed without supper."

DEPUTY DEXTER DIPPE

9

Clackamas County Sheriff's Deputy Dexter Dippe sucked in his gut at the sight of Wanda standing in the doorway, framed top and bottom by strawberry locks and fuzzy pink slippers.

"Deputy Dipp?" She motioned him inside.

"That's Dipp-*ee*," ma'am." His gut popped back out at the sight of Armand standing by the stone fireplace.

"Deputy Dipp-*ee,* meet Inspector François Poulet of Interpol." The two feigned salutes.

"Not so much em*pha*sis on the last syl*lab*le, ma'am," quipped Dippe, tucking in his shirt with deep thrusts. "Besides, all m' friends call me Dex. Rhymes with *sex.*"

"Interesting," snipped Armand.

"*Interpol,* eh?"

"I am on holiday, actually. Chief Cook called me in on this dish. This case."

"Exactly what *is* goin' on?"

"Several attempts on the woman's life."

"Well, I got us this idea," blustered Dippe, puffing out his chest and hiking up his trousers. "Inspector, you hide outside somewhere, an' me'n the lady'll go have coffee for a few hours, an' we'll smoke 'em out that way." He hooked his thumbs on his utility belt. "Now, I know this nice little cafe in Rhododendron, right next t' the motel—"

"My sixth husband, Buck, lives in Rhododendron," she said, smiling sweetly. "He owns the Rhododendron Limb Company."

"I know this nice little restaurant in Boring."

"That's where my first husband, Earnest, lives and works. If you call that work."

"I know this nice little tavern in Brightwood."

"My fifth husband, Ben, is down covering the Brightwood

Slug Festival. Ben Wa, the *newspaper* editor."

"*Slug* festival—?" asked Armand.

"I know this nice little deli in Damascus."

"My fourth husband, General Henri Malaise, runs Damascus Demolition."

"*The* General Malaise—?" asked Armand. She smiled demurely.

Dippe wiped his brow. "Government Camp—?"

"Ugh! That's where *Edgar* lives."

"Timberline Lodge—?"

"Second husband. Six-foot-six."

Dippe scratched the back of his neck. "Just down the road. Ripley's River Resort."

"Third husband."

"Not Rudyard Ripley!" laughed Armand.

"Believe it or not."

Dippe grinned. "I got it, this time I got it!" He picked at a torn cuticle. "There's this nice little bar an' grill down in Sandy."

"Bull," said Wanda.

"I have a rented Ford," announced Armand. "Wanda and I shall meet you in Sandy. Chief Cook and his Volunteers can, as you Americans say, hold down the fort."

"Super!" sang Wanda. "I'll run fetch my coat."

Dippe's face fell . . . then reinflated when Wanda stepped from the walk-in closet wearing a clear plastic raincoat and purple satin pumps.

10

Patrons of the Sandy Bar & Grill broke into spontaneous applause when Wanda walked in. At the sight of the dopey deputy and the suave Swiss, they returned to their fried eggs, short stacks, and pork chops.

"Sandy's got two bars for every grill," quipped Dippe, sliding into the booth beside Armand.

"So?" snickered Wanda, who sat opposite.

"Just trying t' ease the tension, ma'am. The sheriff says we got t' make small talk."

"Foreplay, huh?" tittered Wanda.

Dippe slapped the table and howled with glee. "Just wait'll I tell that t' the sheriff!" He stopped abruptly. "Maybe not."

Armand tapped his fingers impatiently. "Perhaps we should get down to the business."

Dippe shot a sharp glance at Armand. "We got *two* orders o' business, ma'am. First there's the misdemeanor."

"Miss DeMignor—?" inquired Armand.

"*What* misdemeanor?" demanded Wanda.

"Public indecency. We got three hundred an' some-odd phone calls after you appeared on Good Morning Oregon."

"I never appeared—"

"Three hundred an' some-odd taxpaying citizens say you did. They say you go around exposin' yourself t' family men an' innocent children."

"I'm a nudist!"

"Nudidity is against the law."

"Not in Zigzag."

"You're the postmistress, right?"

"The *mail* person."

"What does the Post Office say?"

"Take a bath, comb your hair, brush your teeth, trim your nails, smile—"

"America!" shouted Armand. "The land of the free, and the home of the brave!"

Patrons cheered. Dippe slid down in the booth.

A gum-chewing waitress with vacancy signs in her eyes brought three mugs and filled them with coffee.

"I had a *huge* breakfast," laughed Armand, patting his stomach.

"I'm on a diet," groaned Wanda, smoothing wrinkles from her raincoat.

"Uh … nothin' for me," mumbled Dippe, dragging his eyes from the chalkboard menu behind the counter.

The waitress scuttled away, muttering.

"She should live in Boring," chuckled Armand.

"With Earnest," chortled Wanda.

"This is *serious,*" griped Dippe.

"I should say!" blazoned Armand, raising a forefinger. "If attempted murder is taken lightly, society is doomed!"

"I mean public *nudidity!*" grumbled Dippe. "We don't get one call complainin' 'bout damn attempted murder!"

"Leave her alone, ya big bully!" hooted a patron.

"Better nude than screwed, blued, and tattooed!" jeered another.

The crowd broke into a rousing chorus of cackles, guffaws, horselaughs, and ear-splitting whistles.

Dippe jumped up, threw back his shoulders, puffed out his chest, and marched for the door.

11

Chief Cook moved cautiously about his office, favoring every square inch of his body. Sitting made him want to stand. Standing made him want to sit. He was poised between the two when Ben Wa burst through the door, waving his paper.

"Hot off the press, Mac! Big news today!"

The chief grinned. "So I finally made the front page," he said, plopping onto his chair. "Owwwwww!" He shot to his feet. "Oooooooh!"

"Not you, Mac. Wanda."

"She makes the front page every week. It's been six months since *I* made the front page."

"She's better-looking than you, Mac."

"But you were married to her, Ben. You're supposed to hate her."

"The difference is not great between love and hate. I love Wanda to pieces. I hate Wanda to pieces, too. Here, read the banner."

The bold headline sprang from the page: WANDA BARES ALL!

"What the hell, Ben, that's not news."

"Read the subhead, Mac."

"'The Zigzag Papers . . . local author pens lurid exposé of ex-husbands.' Now *that's* news!"

"Told you."

"Tell me the rest."

"Read the story, Mac."

"What in the hell for? You're standing right here."

"Nobody *reads* anymore. So. Wanda appeared on the Good Morning Oregon show. Talked about The Book of Love. Host asked if a new book's on its way. She spilled the beans. Said

Zigzag Papers is chockablock with dirt about the whole bunch of us."

"Ben, that explains—"

"Why ex-husbands are trying to murder Wanda."

The chief's eyes narrowed. *"You* are an ex-husband."

"But *I'm* not *trying!"*

"What if I just picked you all up and ran you in?"

"Ah. Lawsuits would follow."

"Getting so you can't sneeze. Wait . . . I got a better idea!"

"Change your name to *Ford."* Ben slapped his knee. "That's a good one!"

"We'll get Inspector Poulet to round 'em up, down at Ripley's. He's done that sort of thing hundreds of times. And we'll make 'em *squirm* and *sweat* and *twitch,* until they all confess, and . . . and *you,* Ben, can be a spy."

"Quick recovery, Mac."

"Promise you won't say a word."

"Ahhhh, Mac."

"Don't worry, Ben, you'll get your scoop. And maybe one of them Poolitzers."

"Maybe *two* scoops. Got attempted murders . . . *and* got Zigzag Papers."

"What's she got on you, Ben?"

"None of your your business, Mac!"

"Ben, you're turning red."

"Wanda knows everything about everyone. Even you, Mac."

"I got nothing to hide. Much."

"She knows what come in those plain brown wrappers."

"That's none of her damn business!"

"Ah! Red cheek is on the other face!"

"I still don't get it, Ben. Why would Wanda want to blow the whistle on us? We're like family."

"Mystery to me, Mac. But I'm glad I watched Good Morning Oregon. First time I've seen Wanda in clothes. She's a knockout!"

"Clothes—?"

"She wore a long black opera cape open clear to her belly button, like the one Rhonda wears. The host kept getting something in his eye."

"When's this new book due out?"

"It goes to her publisher next week."

"I'll get Inspector Poulet on it right away. And don't you breathe a word. Promise?"

Ben scuffed his heel on the board floor.

The chief unsnapped his holster.

"Promise!"

WANDA'S SISTER RHONDA

12

Ben discovered his office door ajar. He pushed it the rest of the way open and leaped into the dim room, assuming his best karate posture. Rhonda smiled from the guest chair beside his rolltop desk.

"Where did you come from?"

"The same place as my despicable twin," she snapped, tossing her strawberry locks. "But I have the decency to protect my precious body from prying eyes."

He noted her tent-like attire. "That's very true. But how did you get in?"

She held up a key.

"Ah. Forgot."

"You know, Ben darling, we all have good reason to hate my vile sibling."

"Good reason to love her, too."

"Ha!" she snorted, her face twisted like a bar towel. "Ben, you must stop her from publishing her new book."

"Ah. Zigzag Papers."

"You will be ruined if the truth comes out."

"How do you know the truth?"

"I read her manuscript."

"She *let* you?"

"She was at work."

"How did *she* know the truth?"

"You talk in your sleep."

"So. How do you know that?"

"It's in the book."

"Ah. What to do now?"

"Stop her, Ben. Don't let her finish!"

13

Wanda sensed something was dreadfully wrong. First, her tea tasted bitter. Next, she found herself flat on her back in bed, unable to turn to avoid the drops of water drumming on her forehead.

The dripping stopped. She opened her eyes. Armand smiled down at her.

"What—?"

"Someone attempted to murder you with a Chinese water torture. I suspect Ben Wa."

"But Ben's Japanese."

"Then a Japanese water torture." He untied her.

"But why?"

He handed her *The Zigzag Rag.*

"Lies!"

"You appeared on the television."

"Bull!"

"You wore a long black opera cape."

"I don't own a cape . . . long, black, *or* opera."

"You talked about your new book."

"I'm not writing a new book."

"You wish to expose your former husbands."

"I love my husbands. They're family. Hey, I'm clean, François."

"I see."

"No you don't." She drew him down and kissed his lips. Hours, days, weeks passed. Marrakech. Maracaibo. Cairo. Caracas.

"François . . . marry me! No, don't say a word. Throw off your clothes. *Join* me!"

Armand's arms and legs and shirt and pants and shoes

and socks and shorts and undershirt flew in a frenzy. He stood gasping for breath.

"Now you're a nudist!"

He drew in a deep breath and let it out. "What . . . does a nudist . . . do?"

"Walks around without clothes."

"Why?"

"Because the human body is a thing of beauty and a joy forever."

He glanced down.

"A thing of beauty," she murmured.

"So if this woman was not you—?"

"It was my twin sister. Rhonda."

"Why would she do such a thing?"

"She hates me. She thinks I'm loose. But I think she's uptight."

"I see." He sat beside her on the bed.

"No, you don't!" she laughed, kissing him again.

He returned her kiss. Casanova. Don Juan. Valentino.

"Marry me, François!"

"You don't love me."

"How do you know?"

"You love your husbands."

"I love *you*."

"Prove it."

"Marry me."

"Prove it first."

"Marry me first."

"You are not loose."

"Rhonda is loose."

"You said Rhonda is . . . uptight."

"Uptight on the one hand . . . loose on the other."

"And you are the other way around?"

"I am the opposite of Rhonda."

"You and she are like—"

"Sisters."

"Yes."

"Marry me."

"And become Husband Number Seven?"

"Lucky Number Seven."

"What if I told you I am already married?"

"I can spot a married man a mile away."

"What if I told you I make very little money?"

"A famous detective like you?"

"What if I told you I am a simple sous-chef?"

"Bull! I've watched you in action."

"What if I told you my name is … Armand DuBois?"

"The founder of the Swiss Boy Scouts? You're much too young." She kissed him for ages. "Marry me, *please!*"

"No."

"No one has ever said no before."

"Have you always asked?"

"I have never asked!"

"I … am flattered."

"I feel warm and fuzzy. I want your body close to mine. Your lips on mine. Your—"

"Anybody home?"

Wanda bounced off the bed, pointed Armand toward the bathroom, threw his clothes in after him, and slammed the door. "Depends on who's there," she called coquettishly.

"It's me. Chief Cook."

"Are you alone?"

"Yeah, sure."

"I'm going to count to three, then open the door." She looked back at the bathroom. "One … two … two and a half …"

Armand stepped out, dressed.

"Three!" She turned to open the front door.

He stepped back into the bathroom and pulled the door shut after him.

"Chief Cook! What brings you to my house?"

"The Zigzag Papers."

"François just told me."

"François—?"

She gestured with her head.

He scanned the empty room. "And what did *you*… tell François?"

She whipped around and threw up her hands. "Oh, just that I'm innocent. That I'm not writing a new book. That I *love* him!"

"What about… the plain brown wrappers?"

"*Screw* the plain brown wrappers!"

"Wanda, I've gained a whole new respect—"

"Sit on it!" She whipped back around.

"—for you… but you're in grave danger."

"Tell that to Inspector François Poulet of Interpol!" she shouted, again turning toward the bathroom.

"Hallo!" hailed Armand, bounding up the porch steps.

"Déjà vu," said the chief, stroking his chin.

"Worm!" said Wanda, turning slowly.

"I am very close," announced Armand, "to clearing up the mystery."

"Why… that's why I came over," blustered the chief.

"Bull!" scoffed Wanda.

14

Edgar appeared at the door, his ratty trench coat dry at last.

"I found it!" he tittered, lifting his silvered sunglasses.

"Religion?" she snipped, sticking her tongue out at Armand.

"My eye!" He slapped down a stack of eight-by-ten prints. On top were two shots of Wanda peering through bars. Then a shot of her caught in Edgar's favorite pose.

"Ugh!"

Then, twelve tight shots of Rudyard Ripley's nostrils. Then, a shot of her hanging upside down from a tree. Then, a shot of—

"Buck!" she boomed.

Armand flipped the penultimate photo, exposing—

"Edgar! Without his eye!"

Edgar smirked. "He sent it in for developing . . . to *my* photo lab!"

"Why don't I just round 'em up," prodded the chief.

Armand raised a hand. "First, I shall visit each of these husbands . . . and interrogate."

"I was kinda hoping," the chief moped, "we could just round 'em up. Like in the movies."

"Twenty-four hours," promised Armand, escorting Edgar and the chief to the door. "Now I must interrogate Wanda."

"Not again!" she moaned.

He closed the door, wondering what Uncle Claude would say if he could see his favorite nephew now. Alone behind closed doors with a naked woman who happened to be captivating, desirable, enchanting, fascinating, gorgeous, heavenly, and eager.

"Where do I begin?" she sighed.

"At the beginning . . . with Earnest Hummingbird."

"He's totally weird," she began, dropping to her polar bear

rug. "He's got all these pretty butterflies, thousands of them, mounted in these unnatural positions... with moths and beetles... even their own caterpillars!"

"I see," he sympathized, sinking to the rug beside her.

"He led me to his secret hiding place on our wedding night. He said he wanted to show me his 'little prides and joys.' I expected *anything* but that. 'But don't you see,' he said, 'how delightfully, how deliciously, how delectably, they're doing it?' 'Bull!' I said. 'They're not doing it, they're *dead!*' I came in one time when he had all these little kids in his lab, and he was teaching them to mount butterflies, and I told him, 'It's one thing, what you do in private, but *this* is downright *depraved!*' And he said, 'But this is what I do for a living.' And I said, 'A living what? Certainly not a living butterfly. You couldn't get one to look at you cross-eyed!' The kids got off on that."

"Are you being serious?"

"He even mounted *me* like a butterfly ... which is fine if you're a butterfly. 'Fly like a man,' I told him. Then I realized *I* was beginning to think like a butterfly. So I flew."

"Why did you marry him?"

"He was so gentle."

"I see."

"Then I met Fritz Jerrold, handsome Olympic gold medal skier... virile, charming, yet so helpless. That's when I started The Book of Love. I wanted to try all kinds."

"Of love—?"

"Of men, silly. Take Henri ... General Malaise. Even at ninety-nine, he liked to chase me around a tree. And when I got bored, if he didn't drop first, I'd just let him catch me and kiss me on both cheeks, and that was that. No fuss, no muss."

"Tell me about Rhonda."

"Crap!" she snorted. "I haven't seen her since we were tiny. Even then, she hated me. Even before we were born."

He massaged the base of her neck. "Before—?"

"I knew what she was thinking. I still do."

He began working slowly down her spine.

"Don't stop. I feel sorry for her. Oh, that feels so good. I mean, if you're out there doing it with every man who has a banana, every fruit with nuts, it's like a full course meal served from a blender. *Mmmmmmmmm.* Like warmed-over baby food. *Ooooooooh.* Not very memorable. *Ahhhhhhhhh.* Not tasty at all."

He reached her tailbone.

"Wooooooooooo!"

"Where does she live?"

She flipped over and sat up. "Why are we talking about *her?* She *hates* me!"

"Do you hate her?"

"I don't hate anyone. I love everyone."

"Even Rhonda—?"

"I would if she loved *me.*"

"How are you and she different?"

"I only do it with one man. The one I'm married to. It limits the field, but *woo,* those first few months!"

"And Rhonda—?"

"Rhonda's got round heels. Now, let me tell you about Husband Number Three...."

Later, as Armand drove away, an ominous thought crossed his mind: What if one of Wanda's former husbands dislikes being interrogated?"

EARNEST HUMMINGBIRD

15

"I'd be delighted," said Earnest, ushering Armand into his orange and black spotted cottage on the outskirts of Boring. "I've never been interrogated before."

Armand glanced about the dim room. The knotty pine walls were covered with butterflies mounted in frames of various shapes and sizes. Lifelike butterflies clung motionless to branches in bell jars and display cabinets.

"You killed all those butterflies?" he gasped.

"You should see my laboratory," said Earnest, raising his wire-rimmed trifocals and pinching the bridge of his nose. "Not to mention my … *private* collection." His tiny eyes danced, and his belly, round as a butterball, burbled as he rocked on his heels.

"Yes, I've heard about that," replied Armand.

"Doubtless you read it in Wanda's new book," whimpered Earnest. "In the chapter entitled 'Butterfly Nut.'"

"Wanda is not writing a new book."

"Well, it's not that way. Not at all. And she had no right to tell it … especially on television."

"You saw her?"

"Rhonda saw her."

"You saw Rhonda?"

"I see Rhonda … from time to time."

"And she told you—?"

"Wanda wants to destroy me. To ruin my reputation among my fellow lepidopterists. Prevent Boring boys and girls from mounting butterflies in my laboratory on Saturday mornings, while I guide their inexperienced little hands."

"I see. So you—?"

"Let poison caterpillars loose in her living room!"

"You admit you tried to murder her?"

"Do you realize how many caterpillars that would take? Millions!" Earnest picked up a feather duster and fluttered about the room, flicking bell jars. "Millions and *millions* of poison caterpillars, and I gave Wanda a few hundred at most. Just enough to make her tummy upset."

Armand eased toward the door. "That's all I have."

"Before you leave, Inspector, won't you step into my laboratory?" Earnest swung open a heavy metal door. "I think you will be surprised."

Armand stepped into the pitch-black room. "Where will I find the light—?" The door clanged shut behind him.

"Surprise!" came Earnest's muffled call.

The lights blinked on. Armand gasped. Millions and millions of spiny caterpillars swept in undulating waves across the ceiling, walls, and floor!

"Rhonda warned me you were coming!" Earnest shouted through the door.

The lights blinked off. Concentric stars burst behind Armand's eyes. *"Caterpillars!"* he screamed. "I feel them!" He shook one foot, then the other. Frantically tucking his pant legs into his socks, he danced the way he had seen Gene Kelly dance in an old American movie. *"Sing*-ing in the *rain,"* he sang at the top of his lungs, "just *sing*-ing in the *rain—!"*

The lights blinked back on. The door opened a crack.

Armand spun and yanked the door wide open, jerking Earnest, startled, into the room. Earnest hit the slick where Armand had danced, slid the width of his lab, and crashed into the wall, flattening hundreds of caterpillars.

"My babies!" he sobbed, sinking to the floor, where he flattened dozens more. "These are perfectly harmless little guys! I just wanted to scare the daylights out of you!"

Armand tiptoed from the laboratory along the path Earnest had cleared. "Don't blame me!" he called over his shoulder.

"Who should I blame?" blubbered Earnest.

"Blame Rhonda!"

"My pretty butterfly?" sniffed Earnest. "You must be mad!"

FRITZ JERROLD

16

"Ya, I'm used to it," said Fritz, bumping a plump young blonde from his cast-free knee and motioning Armand into the chair opposite his. *"Wiedersehen,* goodbye now, ski bunny! And ask me anything, I will tell you, Herr Inspektor. Where I come from, we get interrogated all the time."

Armand glanced about the dim, dark wood confines of the Blue Ox Bar. "So ... this is a watering hole."

"Ya."

Armand smiled knowingly. "This is where you *hustle.*"

"Ya?"

"I see."

"Well—?"

"Well ... I mean—"

"What kind of interrogation *is* this? I don't know from what you talk!"

Armand rubbed his temples. "Shall we proceed?"

"Ya!"

"Did you try to murder Wanda?"

"Why should I try to murder Wanda?"

"The Zigzag Papers."

"I don't know from Zigzags."

"Do you know from Rhonda?"

"Rhonda I know from. From time to time." He glanced at his watch. "She should be showing up any minute now."

Armand jumped to his feet. "That's all I have."

"I could give you lessons."

"I know how to ski."

"You don't know how to *interrogate!*"

Laughing, Fritz grabbed his crutches, swung to his feet, and hobbled toward the men's room.

MILO GRAHAM

17

Armand picked a perfect point for eavesdropping, a booth concealed from Fritz's table, yet only a few feet away. But a wild-eyed young man with flushed face and flame-red curls occupied the spot.

"I need this seat!" pleaded Armand.

The young man waved Armand away. "I need it more than *you* possibly could!" he fired back passionately.

Armand gripped the young man's green velvet lapels. "*I* need it for eavesdropping!"

"As do *I!*" riposted the young man.

"I need to eavesdrop on this table here!"

"My goal is one with yours!"

At a sound, Armand glanced toward the men's room door. "Touché!" he croaked, pushing the young man ahead of him as he squeezed into the narrow booth.

The young man reached a hand around. "I am Inspector François Poulet of Interpol," he announced.

"You are . . . *who?*"

"Inspector—"

"I thought you were fiction!" Armand reached up and struggled to shake hands in the tight space, settling for three fingers. "What . . . brings you to Timberline Lodge?"

"I am on a case! And why are *you* here, six thousand feet above the sea, on such a glorious summer's day? What brings *you* to this incomparable snow-clad peak?"

"I, too, am on a case. My name is Armand DuBois."

"Never heard of you."

"Just as well."

"Hold! Fritz returneth!"

"Is this a disguise?" asked Armand, fingering the young

man's wide lace collar and red bow-tied scarf.

"Shhh! You're a terrible eavesdropper!"

No sooner had Fritz settled into his chair than a voice called, "Fritz, darling!"

"That would be Rhonda," whispered Armand.

"Do you want the whole world to know?"

"Rhonda, *Liebchen!*"

"Oh, don't get up, poor dear! Here, I'll pull my chair around."

"Ya, you called?"

"Have you heard? About The Zigzag Papers?"

"Ya... something... but what?"

"Wanda's latest book. She's out to get you, Fritz, and we've got to do something!"

"Ya? What thing?"

"She said, on Good Morning Oregon, which all your young women watch between encounters with their handsome Olympic medalist, 'Fritz Jerrold won't climb the slopes... because chickens don't ski!'"

Fritz pounded the table. "We kill her!"

"Chickens—?' whispered Armand.

"Shhhhhh!" shushed the young man.

"Not so loud, Fritz. Someone might hear."

"She won't get away with this!" he hissed.

"Think, Fritz. There must be something... *easy* you could do. You're so big and strong, I'll bet you could tear Wanda's house to the ground. With *her* in it."

"Ya? And I could twist Wanda's neck like the chicken!"

"Chicken—?" whispered Armand.

"Chicken!" crowed Fritz.

"I hear an echo," said Rhonda. She rose and stepped to the booth where Armand sat looking up, a hand clapped to his mouth.

"Wanda!"

"Wrong."

"Rhonda?"

"Right."

"How silly of me!" he said, forcing a laugh. "You know, without the opera cape, you would look just like—"

"And who are *you?*"

"Armand DuBois."

"You don't say."

"I am Swiss."

"Really now."

"On holiday."

"How nice."

"I was just sitting here with Inspector—" He groped behind his back.

"You are the only inspector here . . . *Inspector.*"

"You will come with us!" ordered Fritz.

18

Armand rose and permitted Fritz to twist his arm. Out the door and up the stairs and across the lobby and in and out among the milling throngs of tourists and up some more stairs and down a long hallway and into a small room, all the while marveling at the splendid stone masonry he had read about in the visitor's guide, the handsome wrought iron railings and hinges, the fantastic wood posts and pillars with native animals carved by artisans during the Great Depression.

"Pretty good pace for a chick—" He bit his tongue. "For someone wearing a cast." He permitted Fritz to tie his arms and legs to a chair.

"Good! Now I will go and blow Wanda's house down!"

"And I will keep Inspector Poulet company until you return. *Wiedersehen,* Fritz darling!"

She bolted the door and circled Armand, throwing back her hood and shaking out her strawberry locks. "I trust you are … comfortable," she said, smiling seductively.

He squirmed. "The rope is uptight."

She laughed. "You mean … *too* tight."

"Yes."

"So—?"

"So make it loose."

"You take me for a sucker?"

"Sucker—?"

"Chump."

He studied her eyes for guideposts. "Noooooo," he said guardedly.

She jerked on the rope. *"Now* is it too tight?"

"Yes!"

"So *suffer.*"

He laughed. "How forgetful! I can prove I am Armand DuBois. My passport!"

"Interpol forges passports. Dozens every day."

"I am hungry."

"No dice."

"Thirsty—?"

"Try horny."

"I am horny."

"Well, I can accommodate you there."

"First … what is horny?"

"Body chemistry. I'm a girl. You're a boy."

"I am … chicken."

"Fancy that! One of my specialties."

19

A sharp rap sounded. Rhonda jumped.

"Who's there?" she said sweetly.

"Bellhop."

"What do you want?"

"I have a message."

"Slip it under the door."

"'Tis an oral message."

"Well, *speak!*"

"Let the door be opened."

"Let the door remain closed."

"House rule. Reveal thyself!"

Armand worked furiously to free his hands as Rhonda slid back the bolt and eased open the door. A lock of curly red hair popped through the crack. She slammed the door.

"Owwwwwwwwwwwwwwwwww!"

Throwing open a window, she climbed out onto the stone ledge and leaped the short distance to the snowbank beneath. "Au revoir . . . *Armand,"* she called as she slipped from sight.

He threw off his ropes and flew to the door, flinging it wide. "Inspector!"

The young man stumbled into the room, clutching a wisp of red hair. "I am undone!" he cried, flopping on the bed.

Armand pulled him to his feet. "If we do not arrive in time, *Wanda* will be the undone one!"

They raced out the door and along the hallway and down the stairs and across the crowded lobby and down more stairs and through the stone arch to the parking lot, Armand raptly absorbing as much of the art, architecture, and craftsmanship as he could. All four tires on his rented Ford were flat.

"We shall take mine!" crooned the young man, ecstatic at

this twist of fate. He sprang to the cracked seat of an old and incredibly battered black Indian motorcycle speckled with blue and white dents. Armand stepped uncertainly into the torpedo sidecar.

Zipping around a hairpin turn, the young man pointed to the south. "Look thither!" he exulted. "Mount Jefferson! And beyond, Mount Washington!" He swept his free hand in a wide arc. "Transcendent spires above a flood of green waves washing the world away!"

They swung into an outside curve. Armand gaped down to where the road emerged, a thousand feet below. Suddenly a bolt popped free!… and another!… and another! The sidecar shook violently. *"Stop!"* he shrieked.

"I can't!" shouted the young man. "No brakes!"

Armand grabbed the handle behind the motorcycle seat. Struggling up and out of the wobbly sidecar, he straddled the cockpit. Another outside curve strained against the one remaining bolt. Scenes of his failed trials at the Swiss Gymnastics Academy flashed before his eyes, his miss on the parallel bars, the mortal agony. Calling on the spirits of his dear departed mother and father—and his Uncle Claude—he propelled himself toward the motorcycle just as the last bolt snapped and the sidecar jumped the guardrail and shot out into space, its wire wheel whistling. He landed hard on the buddy seat and wrapped his arms around the young man's waist. The motorcycle reared up—and stayed up—until they coasted past the stop sign on Highway 26, just shy of Government Camp.

"A new downhill record!" crooned the young man.

Armand wiped tears from his eyes, ears, and nose. "You should have your license taken away!"

"My *poetic* license?"

"Your *driver's* license!"

"First, they must give it back!"

"Ha! You are not Inspector François Poulet of Interpol!"
"And you are not Milo Graham!"
"Who is Milo Graham?"
"*I* am Milo Graham!"
"Who *are* you?"
"Some say a mad poet. Some say ... simply *mad!*"

20

Milo flung himself to the floor and kissed Wanda's feet.

She threw her arms around Armand's neck and kissed his lips.

"Have you seen all my husbands already?" she asked.

"Two is enough," replied Armand.

Milo leaped to his feet. "One is on his way here!" he trilled. "The giant who grinds bones!"

"Listen!" said Armand. They froze. A strange noise rose from beneath the cabin.

"'Tis a cat with asthma!" said Milo.

"Sounds more like somebody using a rusty saw," said Wanda.

"Hark! The cat hath caught a rat!"

"Some rat has just pried a nail."

"Quickly!" said Armand. "Your electric sweeper."

She hauled her vacuum cleaner from a closet.

"Good! Now, cayenne. Do you have it?"

"Tons." She ran to a kitchen cabinet.

Armand removed the dust bag from the canister, plugged in the cord, and dragged the sweeper out onto the front porch.

"Milo, take the hose and find, you know, a breathing hole in the foundation."

"On! Sail on!" piped Milo, vaulting the porch railing.

"Quietly!"

Wanda brought out a large tin of cayenne. Armand emptied it into the canister.

"So much for organic pest control," she said.

"*Au contraire!*" he laughed, connecting the hose to the exhaust and flipping the switch. The sweeper roared to life, pumping pepper through the vent.

HOBO HOOKER

They ran to the back porch and listened. Sneezes and dry coughs drew closer. Armand picked up a broken limb. A head popped out of the crawl space. He dropped the limb.

"That's not Fritz!" exclaimed Wanda.

"Who art thou?" intoned Milo.

Tears coursed down the delicate network of creases lining the man's weathered face. "Hobo Hooker," he wheezed. "You can call me Bo."

"What are you doing under my house?" she demanded.

"I . . . live there," he replied, sneezing.

"You don't mean," said Armand, "you . . . *live* there."

"If you call just fiddling in the woods all day and sleeping under a stranger's house at night *living*."

He stood and brushed dust from his threadbare three-piece suit. "Personally, I prefer to think of it as burning my mortgages behind me."

Milo clapped his hands and beamed. "Hast thou lived there long?"

"Since the start of the second quarter. Moved in April First."

"Impossible!" gasped Wanda.

Bo kicked the bottom step with an open-toed wingtip shoe. "Trying to improve my lot a little. Putting in a pallet so I won't have to sleep on the ground. Guess I gave myself away."

"That's *awful!*" said Wanda, taking Bo by the hands. "If you like, you can stay with me!"

He arched his bushy eyebrows. "I died and this is heaven, right?"

"*Right!*" chimed Milo, throwing himself at Wanda's feet.

"Well, I guess I *could,*" said Bo, scratching his silver chin stubble. "Sorta like being offered a five-for-one stock split in a bull market. But you'll have to keep that bearish sister of yours away."

"Rhonda—?" asked Armand, wide-eyed.

"They fight like middle management."

Armand turned to Wanda. "You say you have not seen your sister—?"

She looked away. "I have not *wished* to see her. But she won't leave me alone."

He paced, puzzling. "Tell me, Mister Hooker—"

"Call me Bo. Never had a real home, and never will."

"Don't *say* that!" cried Wanda.

"Always lived *under* someone, ma'am. Even in the Navy. *Especially* in the Navy. Bunk beds when I was a kid."

He wiped a tear from his eye.

"One transfer after another with the company. On the rods when the bulls rode the open boxcars. Crawl spaces of people's houses. I get by."

"You now have a home, Bo!"

"You mean it? I can move in? With *you?*"

"*Under* me. I mean you can stay."

"Bless you, ma'am. I'll be as quiet as a retired board chair."

"No!" said Armand. "You shall make a terrible racket. You shall ... bark like a dog!"

"Brilliant!" trilled Milo. "And I shall play the staring owl, *tu-whit!*"

"No ... not exactly."

"Who then will set the stage?"

"Shakespeare!"

Milo drew back, bowing. "A thousand pardons—"

"The barking dog," said Armand, "shall keep the sneaking chicken at bay."

"Chicken—?" said Bo.

"A chicken shall attack this place ... unless you bark."

"I'm not real good at barking."

"Can you *howl?*"

"Better'n most hounds! AoooOOOOooooOOOOooo—"

"Good! And Milo, you pace in front of the windows, so Fritz can see you."

"But what am I to *do?*"
"Recite the Sonnets."
"Oh, joy!"

21

"Wanda . . . can you drive Milo's motorcycle?"

She ran inside, reappearing minutes later wearing a clear plastic jumpsuit and black leather motorcycle boots.

Armand climbed on behind her. She whipped the throttle, stomped the starter, ripped the gear shift lever, and popped the clutch. "Hang on!" she shouted as they shot out onto Highway 26.

"Where are you taking me?" he called over the roar.

"You're the one who wanted to go!"

"I want to go to Ripley's!"

"We just passed it!" She spun the motorcycle around and gunned it, spitting gravel from the highway shoulder across all four lanes.

"There are no brakes!" he yelled.

Sparks trailed from her boot heels as they crunched to a stop just shy of Ripley's sign.

"The Last Resort—?"

"This Side of Mount Hood," she laughed. "The bushes need trimming."

He smiled. He was beginning to enjoy this Inspector business. "And now, we must see Rudyard."

She frowned. "I do not wish to see Rudyard."

"We must ask about the cage."

"We know about the cage. Besides, Henri lives here and I don't wish to see him, either."

"General Malaise? We must ask *him* about your car."

"It's obvious. He used too much dynamite. Even in the war he used too much. That's why he was tried and convicted by both sides. He's still wanted by the Swiss."

"The *Swiss*—?"

GÉNÉRAL HENRI MALAISE

"He ran out of bridges before he ran out of dynamite. Switzerland was so close."

An ancient man wearing a dress uniform complete with medals sprang from the brush. *"Voilà!"* he triumphed.

"Henri!" she moaned. Jumping from the seat, she darted toward the main lodge, Henri in hot pursuit. Armand let the motorcycle crash to the driveway and dashed after them.

She circled a large cedar tree whose lower limbs were cut away. Henri shot up the trunk at full tilt and pounced as she passed beneath. "To the victor belongs the spoils!"

"We're not married!" she protested.

He kissed her on both cheeks. *"Et voici!"*

"Henri, you wicked man!"

"And you…you naughty little girl!"

She turned bright red. "Oh no!"

He slapped her bottom. *"Mais oui!"*

Armand rushed up. "General—?"

Henri rose on his toes and tapped his heels, saluting crisply.

"General, we need to speak with you about the bomb."

"It never should have been invented!"

"The bomb in Wanda's car."

"That was no bomb. That was plastique!"

"Henri," said Wanda, softly, "you used too much."

"I was confused."

"You thought my car was a bridge?"

"No-no-no. Rhonda told me—"

"Rhonda—?"

"—to blow it sky-high. She told me you were exposing me. I feel terrible!"

"This means war!" whooped Wanda.

Henri grabbed her hands and danced her in circles on the green. "Hi ho, hi ho, it's off to war we go!"

"What would Uncle Claude say?" mused Armand as Wanda rushed up, short of breath.

"Who . . . is Uncle Claude?"

"My late mother's brother. My teacher at École Hôtelière. The famous chef who employs me."

"The chef you employ—?"

"Yes. Also, my friend. My trusted advisor. My former scoutmaster. My—"

"Does Uncle Claude also not believe in kissing?" Before he could answer, she immobilized him with her lips.

Henri staggered up, leaned against Armand, and saluted. "Bravo! And now . . . back to the front!" He disappeared into the bushes.

Armand disengaged. "Where does Rhonda live?"

"Not more interrogation!"

"Just the one question."

"I don't know."

"How often do you see her?"

"One question . . . ha!"

"The question has . . . parts."

"She shows up when I least expect it."

"Then we must set a trap."

"We've already set one. For Fritz."

"Oh no! Milo and Bo! We must hurry!"

22

Quick blasts of unmuffled exhaust rapped in their ears as they peered through a thicket of thimbleberry bushes. Milo and Bo were nowhere to be seen. Fritz sat in the wire cab of a monstrous Caterpillar tractor, pushing and pulling an assortment of knobbed levers.

The dull yellow machine lurched forward, belching black smoke. The chain circling Wanda's cabin strained for an instant, then flipped its hook and fell with a rippling clank. Fritz idled the engine.

"We must *stop* him!" whispered Armand.

"*You* stop him," whispered Wanda. "He's bigger than both of us."

Fritz jumped down and strode to the cabin, leaving his cast propped on the tractor seat. Raising the chain above the chiseled stone foundation, he pulled in the slack and began working his way to the far corner.

"Now!" said Armand.

"Now *what?*"

"Now we steal the tractor!"

"Fritz can run faster than the tractor."

"Then we steal the key."

"He can run faster than either of us."

"He cannot catch both of us."

"He's not trying to murder you."

"I shall create a diversion while you escape."

"Bull! I can't even outrun Henri in these boots."

"Too late! Here comes—"

"AoooOOOOoooOOOOooo OOOOoooOOOOooo!"

Dropping the chain, Fritz cocked an ear. "Ya?" he said. "Pooch?"

"AoooOOOOooo!"

"Here, pooch!" He dropped to his knees and peered through a vent. "Here, poochie-pooch! Come on, come to Fritzy!"

"AoooOOOO … oooOOOO … oooOOOO!"

"Poor poochie!" Jumping up, he ran to the back porch and somehow managed to squeeze into the narrow crawl space opening. "Poochie-pooch—?"

Armand and Wanda sank to the ground.

"*Now* what?" she asked.

"Now we rescue Bo."

"How?"

"One question at a time."

"Owwwww … owwwwww!"

They leaped up. "That's not Bo!" she said. "Follow me!"

She charged up the back steps, whisked a spool of heavy twine from a shelf and flew over the railing, landing inches from where Fritz's feet protruded, Armand hot on her heels, breathing hard. She hog-tied Fritz before he could say, "What—!"

"AoooOOOOoooOOOOooo!"

"Oh, shut up!" muttered Fritz.

Milo, feverishly radiant, stepped out onto the porch. "Snatches of Wanda," he warbled.

"Milo!" she exclaimed.

He bowed with a great flourish. "When softly steals the ebon cloak … down Wanda's cheeks and round her heel … full well her form reveals the yoke … of years spent grinding at the wheel!"

She blushed.

He beamed.

"Five times a night she bolts her door … and whispers words to speed release … from fantasies spun 'round the whore … in tribute to her golden fleece!"

She stood transported.

He pursued.

ANNA GRAHAM

"Ten times a day she toots her horn…and blows the sun a kiss in thanks…for heavenly body and soul reborn…well-balanced on the books of banks!"

"Woo!" said Wanda.

"Bravo!" shouted Armand.

"AoooOOOOoooOOOOoooOOOOoooOOOO!"

"Thank you!" rhapsodized Milo, blowing kisses left and right. "And for my next selection—"

"Milo Graham!"

Milo shrank to a fetal position as his sister rushed up. "Anna!" he squeaked.

"Milo, I have worried for you *everywhere,* trying not to be searched!"

"Waning is an awkward word—"

"A telephone pole found the medicine on top of your sidecar, and it's way past the police to take your time!"

"—when waxed about the moon."

"I have prepared home, so come, please fettuccini with me." She led him away.

Armand and Wanda looked at each other with a mixture of merriment and wide wonder.

"May I take a turn now?" asked Fritz.

"*You* write poetry?" asked Wanda.

"I have something to say," he said. "I don't mean to be a meanie. I went, you know, *crrrrazy.* Wanda, I *love* you!"

She untied his feet, and, with Armand's help, pulled until he popped free.

"Thank you so much," he said, stretching to his full height and working his arms and legs like a rusty puppet. "Now, about the pooch…"

"It is Hobo Hooker," said Armand. "He lives beneath the house."

"Oh ya. Then we leave him. And I guess I take the Cat back." He leaned down and stuck his head through the crawl space opening. "Bye-bye, Hobo."

"Bye-bye," said Bo.

Fritz hit his head. "That's some pooch!" he exclaimed.

23

"Will you stay?" asked Wanda. She had traded her motorcycle boots for beaded moccasins and now sat cross-legged on her polar bear rug, weaving a daisy chain.

Armand sat facing her. "I have three husbands yet to go," he replied.

"Marry me, François!"

"How can you think of marriage when your own sister is doing these terrible things?"

"Screw Rhonda! I *love* you, François!"

"Mostly, I think I love you back."

"Mostly—?"

"I love you back, but—"

"But—?"

"I cannot put my finger on it."

"I won't ask you again." She leaned forward and placed the woven ring of daisies on his head. "Watch out for Buck. Rudyard and Ben are pussycats, but Buck is a saber-toothed tiger. He thinks we're still married."

BUCK FULLER

24

"Yeah, I mind very much!" Buck bellowed from inside his double-wide mobile home. "A lot, in fact!"

"I just want to talk—"

"I don't talk to foreigners!"

"Five minutes."

"Not one damn second!"

"Why not?"

"You're not a native."

"Are you?"

"Damn right!"

"May I ask which tribe?"

"What're you, a wise guy?"

"Yes. No! Now … do you know Rhonda?"

"Sure. I mean, she *is* my sister-in-law."

"Do you see her? From time to time?"

"So what if I do?"

"I should like to learn of your relationship."

"You looking for a knuckle sandwich?"

Armand hesitated. "No." He heard a snicker. "Is there someone with you?"

"I'm a married man. That was my … canary."

The canary snickered again.

"That's all I have," said Armand, turning to leave. He heard the door bang open and slam shut. He froze, trying to envision a knuckle sandwich.

"Hold on there, foreigner!"

Swallowing hard, Armand turned back, dropping his eyes from where a menacing head should have loomed to where a round, baby-faced head sat at belt-buckle height. "You're much smaller than I thought," he said.

"Wanna make something of it?"

"Make something—?"

"Yeah, well, I'd make mincemeat outta you!"

"Mincemeat—?"

"But look . . . man to man, I don't want you running to Wanda with some cock-and-bull story about me . . . messing around. Get my drift?"

"Messing around—?"

"I mean, we all like a little on the side."

"I see."

"So be a pal. Lie."

"First . . . why did you try to murder Wanda?"

"She's been seeing another man!"

"A little on the side?"

"Naw, that's what men do."

"What do women do?"

"Cheat!"

"So you . . . *mess around* . . . with women who *cheat*."

"Yeah. No! You looking for a fat lip?"

"No!"

"Just what *are* you looking for?"

"The truth."

"Yeah? Well, you won't find it around here!"

An idea popped into Armand's head. "Tell me about your business," he said, striking a casual pose. "I should like to learn about the Rhododendron Limb Company."

Buck grinned. "Now, that's a subject I can warm to!" He led Armand to a rusted Quonset hut and ushered him in. "So you see," he said, pointing to a string of faded photos taped to the corrugated wall, "we strip the limbs off ugly Christmas trees and then put 'em back on, only even. You can keep your trunk stored away, year after year, and just pick up a fresh batch of limbs."

"Fascinating," said Armand, who listened with half an ear

as he formed a surefire strategy.

"Some folks, of course, like this collapsible aluminum model. We can spray it any color. Even flock it."

"*Flock* it—?"

Buck switched on an air compressor. "Here, watch this." He picked up a spray gun and adjusted the nozzle.

Armand sensed the time was right. He would admit to being the man Wanda was seeing, but claim it was Rhonda he really wished to see. To keep him from seeing Wanda, Buck would then tell him the whereabouts of Rhonda. "I am the other man—"

"Damn foreigner!" snorted Buck, flocking Armand from head to toe.

25

"I have been expecting you, Inspector," said Ben, ushering Armand into the modest office of *The Zigzag Rag*. "But not expecting your disguise. Please, take a load off."

Armand sat, shedding a ring of pink fluff. "You know why I am here," he said.

"You seek a clue."

"I seek an answer."

"To the question of why someone tried to murder Wanda."

"To the question of why *you* tried to murder Wanda."

"Ah. The water torture didn't fool you."

"It was a *Chinese* water torture."

"But *I'm* not *Chinese*."

"You are the only Asian among her husbands."

"So. My subtle ploy didn't work."

"Rhonda got you to do it. Right?"

"You're pretty smart, Inspector."

"It is my job."

"Ah. But you're wrong. It's not Rhonda. It's what Wanda's writing in her new book."

"There is no new book."

"Not true. I saw Wanda on Good Morning Oregon."

"What if Rhonda was the one you saw?"

"You're *very* smart, Inspector."

"Thank you."

"Except Wanda and Rhonda are as different as Yin and Yang. I was married to one . . . and *see* the other, from time to time. Definitely not Rhonda."

"But Wanda does not own a black—" Milo's words flashed through his mind: *When softly steals the ebon cloak—*

"Mister Wa, please tell Chief Cook to round 'em up."

"Going to gather ex-husbands at Ripley's?"

"You, too, are pretty smart."

"It was I who found out you are Inspector Poulet."

Armand's jaw dropped. "How—?"

"I saw your postal card to Uncle Claude and broke the secret code."

Armand suppressed a smile. "I shall have to inform Uncle Claude. Meanwhile, tell Chief Cook eight o'clock in the main dining room."

"Bet you Ripley won't like this."

"Ripley's not in a position to argue."

26

"I say!" raged Rudyard. "You can't do that!" He paced furiously, eyeing the helpers who scuttled about placing fresh red rose-buds in cut crystal vases on impeccably set linen tablecloths. "We have reservations for two hundred!"

"You dropped the cage on Wanda."

Rudyard stopped pacing. "How the *deuce* do you know *that?*" he demanded, smoothing the black satin lapels of his crimson velvet smoking jacket.

"I am not Inspector François Poulet of Interpol for nothing."

"I admit it. But I merely meant to *capture* her, don't you see?"

Armand thought for a moment. "No."

"Conquest is my game . . . and she simply refuses to be conquered. Here, step into my office."

Armand followed Rudyard into a large oak-paneled room made small by the dead creatures whose mounted heads lined the walls. White rhino, Kodiak bear, Bengal tiger, Cape buffalo, African elephant, Rocky Mountain goat, Roosevelt elk, Nile crocodile, Komodo dragon, and on around.

"You killed all these animals?" gasped Armand.

"Well, actually, someone else did the . . . dirty work. But *I* brought them down!"

"How?"

"Hypnotism."

Armand suppressed a laugh. "You dangled a pocket watch—?"

Rudyard tugged at the tip of his nose. "I have," he sniffed, "perfected a technique for mesmerizing animals. Take that rhino. Weak eyesight. Quite a challenge, but I rose to it. Soothed him with my voice. Took the better part of an afternoon, but I had him sleeping like a baby."

"You murdered them in their sleep—?"

"Someone else . . . dispatched them."

"Why?"

"Good grief! *Trophies,* naturally!"

"You wanted Wanda's head on your wall—?"

"Don't be ridiculous! I wanted nothing more than a chance to . . . *charm* her."

"So someone else could . . . *dispatch* her."

"You're treading a fine line, Inspector. One more such affront and I shall be forced to ask Miss Luce . . . Marva . . . to deal with you."

"Who is Miss Loose Marva?"

"Miss Marva Luce."

"You said Loose Marva."

"I don't care!" Rudyard yanked a velvet cord and a wall panel swung open, bull moose and all, revealing a cube-shaped room in which everything—clothing racks, fixtures, implements whose uses defied the imagination, implements whose uses were all too obvious—was made of rubber. Marva sat at the center of the room on a rubber throne.

"Scum!" she snapped, licking Armand's nose with the tip of her whip.

He turned. Rudyard stepped out and slammed the wall panel shut.

"Dance!" snarled Marva, cracking her whip.

Armand danced as if millions of caterpillars crawled up his legs. *"Sing*-ing in the *rain,* just *sing*-ing in the—!"

"Stop!" she shrieked, dropping the whip and clapping her hands to her ears.

He stared blankly. *What have I done?* he wondered.

She picked up the whip. "I told you to *dance!"*

Again Armand danced. *"Sing*-ing in the *rain—"*

"Stop!" she screeched, collapsing on her throne like a punctured balloon.

"—just *sing*-ing in the *rain,* what a *won*-der-ful *fee*-ling, I'm *hap*-py a-gain—"

Rudyard hurriedly swung open the panel and dragged Armand through the office and out into the hallway.

"That," he railed, "was *the* most brazen display of *ill breeding* I have *ever* witnessed!"

"Now," said Armand, "about the dining room—"

"Highway robbery," groused Rudyard, glaring hawkeyed down his aquiline nose. "One corner … but no more!"

"The corner by the stone fireplace."

"That's where our steadiest clientele—"

"Sing—"

"Drat!" grumped Rudyard, wagging the waxed tips of his moustache. *"Double* drat."

27

Marva donned her green wetsuit and dashed to the deep hole above the rapids, snorkel in one hand and explosive-tipped speargun in the other. Her rubber underwater watch read five minutes to six.

"Six grown men," she muttered between clenched teeth, "and not *one* can do a simple job. Well, this is one fish that's headed for the frying pan!" Adjusting her face mask, she jumped in.

At ten after, exhausted from fighting the current, she crawled out and sprawled on the bank. A figure in a black cloak stole from a cluster of rhododendrons.

"Marva—?"

Marva shot to her feet. *"You!"* she fumed.

"I'm Rhonda."

"Tell me another one!"

"Wanda's twin sister. Rudyard and I—"

"Argggh!" Marva broke her speargun in three places.

"I hate my sister," said Rhonda, giving the words a sinister twist.

Marva eyed her suspiciously. "You do—?"

"It was I who inspired the attempts on her life."

Marva tried to coax forth a smile. Failing at that, she produced a gravelly chuckle. "Sit right down!"

Rhonda floated to the ground on her billowing cloak. "I want all six of Wanda's husbands," she said. "I just don't want to be married to them."

Marva plopped back down. "Can't say I blame you. Men are such disgusting creatures."

"Only when you're married to them."

"That I wouldn't know. I've only *owned* them."

"We could work together."

"Hatch a little plot?"

"One that won't fail."

"You're speaking my language. Matter of fact, your sister's going to be at Ripley's tonight. All because that sniveling, spineless Rudyard let Inspector Poulet off the hook. Can you be there?"

Rhonda shook her head. "I . . . I'm not sure—"

"Well, *be* sure! What kind of murderer *are* you if you can't show up for the *murder?*"

"I'll be there."

"You got a gun?"

"No . . . but doesn't Rudyard keep one?"

"*That* thing? We need a *real* gun. One with bullets."

"You get the gun."

"Guns don't come in rubber."

"How about a knife?"

"Don't get cute on me!"

"A club—?"

"Wait! I've got it! At eight-ten on the dot, you sneak into the dining room and turn off the lights. The master switch is next to the kitchen. I'll come down the chimney, and together we'll grab her, wrap her in a tablecloth and haul her off to my secret, sound-proofed chamber, where we can take care of her . . . at our leisure."

"Won't Rudyard suspect?"

"He wouldn't *dare!*"

"Then I'll see you at eight-ten."

"In the dark!"

28

Anna answered the door. "Inspector Poulet, what a pleasant see! Nice to surprise you."

"Yes. Is Milo at home?"

"He's incredible now. But he told me the most resting things about you!"

"Incredible—?"

"You're a beautiful profession, and a human being to your credit."

Armand blushed. "Yes. Well—"

"If you wish me to do it and wake my brother, I shall fly."

"Pardon—?"

"If you wake me and wish to do it—"

"Oh yes. Oh no, that will not be necessary. Just tell him I wish to see him at Ripley's at eight o'clock."

She smiled winsomely. "You can drive on it. I'll bank him myself!"

29

Dinner guests gawked in the soft light as the odd procession snaked through the maze of tables packing the parquet floor. Some sat with soup spoons poised at parted lips, others with knives and forks frozen in ludicrous poses, this one with half-chewed food tucked in a chipmunk cheek, that one with an elbow dipped in the house dressing.

Rudyard led the way, waving the rubber riding crop he borrowed from Marva's private room for the occasion, and tipping his fifty-mission pith helmet to the guests. Wanda smiled atop her purple satin pumps. Fritz sported a fresh cast. Earnest fluttered an enormous butterfly net. Ben toted microphone and tape recorder.

Buck wore a black and green plaid shirt, red suspenders, frisco jeans, hard hat, and wool work socks, having been forced by a bug-eyed Rudyard to remove his caulk boots just shy of the parquet floor. Anna glowed in her taffeta and chiffon high school formal. Milo beamed in his polka dot smock and bouffant beret.

Edgar boasted a new trench coat. General Malaise marched smartly in his freshly pressed dress uniform, six rows of medals gleaming. Chief Cook kept his twelve Zigzag Volunteers, who tended to wander off, corralled.

Armand waited beside the great stone hearth, bathed in the bright beam of a spotlight, a suitcase at his feet.

After pointing everyone to a chair, Rudyard joined him. "Inspector," he confided behind his hand, "there appears to be an extra place."

"It is Rhonda's," replied Armand.

"You don't actually believe she'll show her face."

"I am certain of it."

"Well, *I* most certainly wouldn't!" sneered Rudyard. He plopped onto a chair and promptly crossed his arms and legs.

The room buzzed as diners reluctantly returned to their meals, sneaking peeks between bites, and speculating openly with anyone who would lend half an ear.

Armand stepped to the center of the hearth. *"Murder—"* The room fell silent.

"—is why I have called you all here tonight."

A fork clattered to the parquet floor.

Anna rose. "May I be innocent? I am excused!"

"Pardon!" said Armand, raising his hands and his voice. "The topic is *attempted* murder."

Anna sat back down, biting her lip.

"Foul deeds will rise!" spouted Milo.

Armand continued: "Seven attempts have been made on Wanda Fuller's life . . . one each by her former husbands—"

The husbands cast sidelong glances.

"—and one by a person, or *persons,* unknown."

The others twitched and fidgeted.

Buck jumped up on his chair and stood on tiptoes. "Yeah, yeah," he bellyached, "we know all that!"

Ben rose slowly. "So. Why are we sitting here?"

"Ya," frumped Fritz. "We won't do it again, so—"

"Patience," begged Armand. He pulled a black hooded opera cape from the suitcase.

Wanda gasped. "That's *Rhonda's!*"

"Here," he said, offering her the cape. "Put it on."

"But I don't *want* to put it on!" she cried, pushing it away. "I'm a *nudist!*"

Armand slipped the cape around her shoulders. She shuddered. "Now," he said, "we are going to hear a full confession from each husband."

The six husbands groaned as one. Scattered applause broke out around the room. Buck dropped like a shot. Ben sank like a ship, stern first. "I can see the headline now," he burbled. "Free Zigzag Six!"

"We are going to start with Rudyard."

Earnest wigwagged his hands. "But," he sniveled, *"I am* Wanda's *first* husband!"

"Rudyard is her first attempted murderer."

"My caterpillars had to come from Cambodia! They were delayed in Customs!"

"Oh, shut up!" sniped Rudyard.

Earnest shrank. The others shifted in their chairs.

Rudyard cleared his throat and motioned for silence. No one stirred. "I was driven," he said at last, his voice tranquil, his manner sedate, "by the purest of motives—"

He rocked as he spoke, and softly clicked his heels, and soon those closest, and finally those in the farthest reaches of the room, swayed like metronome wands to the lilt of his velvety voice. "—and my eyes received her beauty as the faithful find fulfillment—"

The lights flickered. The room plunged like a night train into a tunnel. Total darkness.

"Damn!" thundered Rudyard. "Not now!"

Flames erupted from the simulated logs on the fireplace grate, revealing Rudyard crouched at the gas control. "Please, oh *please,*" he pleaded, "resume your pursuit of the siren's call!"

"Aieee*EEEEeeeEEEEeeeEEEE!*"

"I say!" he said, shooting glances left and right.

"Turn that damn thing off!"

He cocked an ear and peered up the chimney. "Marva?"

"Dildohead!" she shrilled. "Turn it off!"

He turned it down.

"I'm going to skin you alive!"

He turned it back up. "You're going to what?"

"Turn it off!"

He turned it back down.

"I'm going to skin—!"

Up.

"AieeeEEEEeeeEEEE!"

Down.

The smell of singed rubber drifted through the dining room.

"Now, what is it you're going to do?"

"I'm going to ... I'm going to ... "

"Give me fifty percent of everything?"

"Over my dead body!" she squawked.

Up.

"AieeeEEEE!"

"Down.

"Damn you ... all right!"

"There are over two hundred witnesses here, if you include the help. Say, 'I do solemnly swear ...'"

"I do *not* solemnly swear!"

Up.

"I *do* solemnly swear! *I-do-I-do-I-do!*"

Down.

"That you, Rudyard Ripley..."

"What is this?"

Up.

"That-you-Rudyard-Ripley!"

Down.

"Are joined with me this day..."

"Are joined... with me... this day..."

"As a full and equal partner..."

"Awww, have a heart!"

"Say it!"

"As a full and... and..."

"Equal."

"Equal."

"Partner."

"Partner."

"So help me..." He scratched his head.

"So help me *what?*"

"What's more important to you than money?"

"Rubber!"

"Say it!"

"So help me... rubber."

The lights came back on. Everyone blinked. Rudyard shut off the gas. The Zigzag Volunteers rushed to assist Marva from the fireplace. The bottom half of her wetsuit smoldered.

<h1 style="text-align:center">31</h1>

Armand waved his arms until the room quieted to a murmur.

"Now . . . Wanda, will you please step forward?"

She remained in her chair. He walked to her and slipped the cloak from her shoulders.

"Wanda?"

"Yes?"

"Will you please rise and step forward?"

"Sure." She rose, stepped to Armand's side, and turned.

"Wanda, why did you switch off the lights?"

She frowned. "Cut the crap, François!"

"You walked to the control panel—"

"Bull!"

He slipped the cape around her shoulders. "Why did you switch off the lights?"

She smiled. "We were going to *eradicate* her."

"Who?"

"Wanda!"

Everyone gasped.

"Who besides you?"

"Marva Luce."

Marva dropped to her knees and beat her fists on the parquet floor.

Armand leaned close. "Rhonda?" he said softly.

"Yes?"

He removed the cape. "Wanda?"

"Yes?"

"Did you know Rhonda was attempting to murder you?"

"My own sister?"

"She made your former husbands try."

"They didn't *really* try. Henri used too much plastique, but otherwise—"

He whipped the cape around her. "Why were you trying to murder Wanda?"

She scowled. "Wanda is so lucky. They all want to marry her. Me, they just want to use."

"What do *you* want?"

"Love."

Again he removed the cape. "Why did you divorce your husbands?"

"I *love* my husbands."

"Why did you—?"

"Because *they* don't love *me!*"

"How do you know?

"Because they all . . . want . . . Rhonda."

"You *are* Rhonda."

"No!"

"Yes! You are Wanda, on the one hand, and Rhonda, on the other."

"I am . . . I *am!* I'm Wanda *and* Rhonda! But how—?"

Milo rushed forth and knelt at her feet. "'Tis mine to explain, fair lady!"

Wanda shook her head, bewildered.

"You are both! The beautiful seductress, and the mate. The open, warm, and loving wife, *and* the concubine. I see you thus in all my waking dreams, and love you more for *everything* you are!"

Anna ran to his side. "Milo, is that *you* speaking? A strong, assertive person in the guise of one I swore on our dear Mama's deathbed to protect against the harsh realities of a cruel world . . . if need be, to my dying breath?"

He embraced his sister. "And you, Anna . . . are you thus freed of your impediment, that you can now speak freely and go about living your life as you so please?"

Anna flung herself at Armand. "*Inspect* me, Inspector!"

"Where do I begin?" he said, caressing her cheek with a hesitant hand.

Wanda flung herself at Milo.

"*You,* my mad poet, are the most ravishing creature in all creation!"

"And *I,*" said Milo, sweeping her into his arms, "am yours at last!"

Diners cheered. Some crushed crackers and tossed the crumbs like confetti, some sailed celery stalks across the room, some spilled soup, and all shook hands and hugged.

"Let the bubbly flow!" Rudyard scolded the help. And the bubbly flowed. And the help helped themselves.

In through a window flew Hobo Hooker, bow in hand and fiddle at chin. "Let's have a hootenanny!" he hollered. Folks gathered round to stomp and shout.

Chief Cook hoisted his pant legs and danced a sprightly hornpipe on the hearth while the Zigzag Volunteers slapped and laughed themselves silly.

Ben dashed here and there, tape recorder at the ready, catching the second halves of exchanges left and right, so profound were the first. "Two scoops and a Pulitzer!" he shouted periodically.

Edgar confessed it was he who had tampered with Wanda's antigravity boots. He set about making amends by shooting everyone—*whirrr-click*—free of charge.

Earnest fluttered about the room a step ahead of Marva, who grinned ear-to-ear in her linen tablecloth toga.

Fritz shot champagne corks at the crystal chandeliers, to giggles and adoring sighs from a cluster of pink-cheeked snow bunnies. Buck took up with the doe-eyed daughter of a Boring baker. And General Malaise, and all the rest, forgot their troubles and just got happy.

FRANÇOIS POULET

Epilogue

1 July

Dear Uncle Claude, these past days in Zigzag have changed my life. I have gained much food for thought, with little thought for food. (I have lost three kilos!) I am taken for Inspector Poulet of Interpol, of all the things. A naked woman falls in and out of love with me, preferring a poet. I fall in and out of love with the poet's sister—out because she prefers to be dominated. And so, off she goes with her Teutonic ski instructor. The naked woman's first husband, who believes he is a butterfly, wins the hand of the rubber maid, who, it turns out, wishes to be mounted with delicacy. I could go on and on. Let me close by saying, please inform the hotel I shall not return to work Thursday next, or ever! My fame as a detective spreads, and I have, just this day, accepted my second case. More when there is more.

Love, François

DAVID HEDGES

JIM AGPALZA

Author's Notes

I wrote *The Zigzag Papers* in 1976 and never submitted it to a publisher. But every few years I'd drag it out and enjoy a laugh or two. I loved my comical characters and their silly actions.

Several months ago, I decided it was high time to see it in print, so I commissioned illustrator Jim Agpalza, creator of the hilarious (in my eyes) cover of my last book, *Trump Über Alles: Rhymes for Trying Times,* to imagine the sixteen characters in this book. He came through with flying colors, capturing them down to Earnest Hummingbird's butterfly bowtie.

When a work is this old, it's bound to be at least a bit out of step with the times. I owe a debt of gratitude to my proofreader, Valerie Witte, and good friend, Lila Wright, for educating me on how current culture differs from that of the mid-1970s.

I can't recall who first suggested that writers get rid of their "precious"—the lines or devices they can't live without—because usually they do more damage than good. Thus it was that I translated heavily accented dialogue into plain English.

The result is that Fritz Jerrold and Ben Wa are now people, rather than cardboard cut-outs. General Henri Malaise is another matter. He's comedic, even without the accent.

I would love to see *The Zigzag Papers* performed on a small stage by an improv group. It's a burlesque, after all. Let the actors run with their interpretations. If nudity offends, Wanda can always wear a tunic with a naked woman painted on it. A high school friend wore such a garment to our class reunion and got a lot of laughs.

David Hedges
Oregon City
January 9, 2023

www.ingramcontent.com/pod-product-compliance
Lightning Source LLC
Chambersburg PA
CBHW040542170726
48295CB00012B/562